The Nanny Diaries #3

Mindy Cummings

Copyright © 2021 by Darling Coxx
All rights reserved. This book or any portion thereof may not be reproduced or used in any manner whatsoever without the express written permission of the publisher except for the use of brief quotations in a book review.

Printed in the United States of America

ISBN: 9781952422126
First Printing, 2021

DarlingCoxx@gmail.com
Instagram: @DarlingCoxx
OnlyFans: @DarlingCoxx
Twitter: @DarlingCoxx

This is a work of fiction. Names, characters, businesses, places, events, locales, and incidents are either the products of the author's imagination or used in a fictitious manner. Any resemblance to actual persons, living or dead, or actual events is purely coincidental.

Chapter One

Dear Diary,

It's been several years since I kept a journal, but I figured writing everything down like this might help me make sense of some things to figure out what to do. I've basically had the same job for six years now although it has changed quite a bit since I started. It's beginning to look like it's time to leave here and start a career, but who's to say that's the right choice.

Mark and Cynthia Jacobs first hired me as a babysitter soon after their son was born. It was for an occasional evening here and there when I was in high school. As time went on, I watched him more and more. The summer after my freshman year of college Cynthia died in a car wreck. It was so unexpected and difficult for the family. She was an amazing person.

There had never been a need for a nanny before because Cynthia didn't work. Most wives who had husbands earning what Mark did would still hire a nanny to stay free for their social calendar. Not Cynthia. Their son was everything to her, and she wanted to be there for all of it.

After she passed away, he needed someone while he was at work. It was supposed to be temporary. At first, it was only until the end of the summer. It would take time to interview and background check possible candidates for the job. It turned into continuing through the fall semester while I took evening and online classes. Then, I was needed more in the evenings as well. Before I knew it, I was graduating college after a senior year of online only classes because sometimes Mark needed me in the evenings.

This is the time when I should be sending out a resume and trying to begin my life. Somehow, I've been suckered in to a live-in nanny position at the Jacob's household. It's temporary for the summer to see if I want to continue to stay on or not.

There's so much to consider. The house is gorgeous. The pay is well above what the average live-in nanny makes. But where is the time for me? I get Sunday's off and the occasional Saturday. Basically, if Mark isn't too busy, I can have the day off.

Meanwhile, I already suspect Chad is cheating on me. I can't pinpoint anything specific, but I feel it in my gut. We started off hot and heavy. We were in love and had a life together ahead of us. I kept pulling away from him by giving so much of myself to this family. He didn't see me on campus anymore, and I wasn't able to attend most of the parties like he did. Sometimes I wonder why he hasn't dumped me yet. Maybe he's hoping I'll quit my job, or worse. I wonder if he's hoping I'll wind up dumping him, so he won't have to be the bad guy. Instead I'm going to be telling him that I'm staying on at least for the next three months.

I debated all day about whether to tell Chad first thing or to wait until nearer the end of our date. Part of me really wanted to do it, and get it over with already. It was going to cause a fight and possibly the official end of our relationship. To be honest, a phone call would be better if that's the case.

Instead, I drove over to his apartment thinking we were headed out to see a local band at one of our favorite bars. Chad had other plans. I definitely couldn't break the bad news to him then. Not when I had a mouth full of cock.

I gave the apartment door a quick knock then opened it and hollered out, "Hello?"

Chad answered from down the hall, "Back here."

Typical of him to not be ready. That's why I started meeting him here instead of having him pick me up. He notoriously always ran late, and this way I could still spend time with him instead of eyeing the clock waiting on him.

As I walked to his room, I expected one of two things. If I was lucky, he'd be showered, but not completely ready to go yet. Mostly,

I figured he'd still be on the damn gaming console wearing the same clothes he had on yesterday and smelling like it too. Nothing would've made me guess I'd find him lying flat on his back in his bed, fully naked with a hard on greeting me, but damn, I do love surprises.

I stood in the doorway absolutely shocked for a minute. My mouth was on the floor. It was the first time Chad had ever done anything like this. He was always a sex with the lights off kind of guy. Changes in sexual likes is a warning, but my mind wasn't looking for signs of a cheater. It was sorely focused on his six inch woody staring back at me.

"Well, you just gonna stand there all night, or are you going to join me?" he laughed.

I bit my lower lip and bounded toward the bed.

Chad held his hand up, and said, "Wait. There is a dress code. You must be nude to join me. Strip."

A grin spread across my face. I was loving this. I started to unfasten the sleeveless button up I was wearing when he stopped me again.

"No, no, no. I said strip," he emphasized. Then he reached over and pushed play on his phone that was connected to the speaker. Music started flowing out.

I chuckled and shook my head.

It was a little out of my comfort zone, and Chad knew that. Still, I had to play along. I started with the buttons again only this time I swayed a little to the music. He smiled and cheered me on even if I'm not the world's best dancer.

Soon, I was getting into it. I started grinding my hips around and teasing as I lowered my shirt little by little. Then onto my skirt. I circled around while rolling my hips as I eased it off me as slow as I could manage. When I kicked it from my feet, I saw Chad was stroking himself. No fair to start without me.

Once I seductively took my bra off and kicked off my sandals, I shimmied back to the wall and leaned against it. Instead of stripping down my panties, I eased my hand inside to start rubbing myself. Chad's eyes widened, and he began stroking himself faster. I continued to gyrate with the music while rubbing my clit. My breathing became shallower, and it wouldn't be long before I started to cum. I arched my back out from the wall and closed my eyes while I moaned.

I felt one of Chad's hands cup my chin and his other rested on my waist. When I opened my eyes, his face was inches from mine. "Strip," he repeated, demanding it.

Not taking my eyes off of his, I lowered my panties to the floor and kicked them away. Chad took half a step back and looked my body over from top to bottom. Then he put both hands on my shoulders and gently pushed down telling me he wanted me to lower myself. Ever the obedient girl, I got on my knees and gave his cock the attention it desired.

I took his shaft in both hands and admired it. Chad's member was a thing of beauty. I allowed my mouth to moisten with saliva then slowly spread it over his knob. I sucked him hard then backed off to lube his whole shaft. Taking his full length in my mouth, I cupped his balls with one hand and played with my clit with the other. As I bobbed on his shaft, I stared into his eyes as much as possible because I knew it drove him crazy.

There's only one thing he liked more than watching me deep throat him. I pulled far back and allowed his cock to slip from my mouth. I started stroking him with my hand and took his balls into my mouth. Only a few seconds passed before he pushed back on my shoulders for me to stop. It wouldn't take much for him to cum like that.

Before I could go back to sucking his cock, he reached down and grabbed me under my arms to help me stand up. He pushed me back against the wall and attacked my breasts. While his mouth tore at one nipple with his teeth, his hand would pinch the other. He switched off on them for a couple minutes until I was about to throw him on the bed and take him.

Chad put his hands on my waist and lifted me up. "Wrap your legs around me," he instructed.

Once I did, he leaned me into the wall and guided his cock into my pussy. Sheer ecstasy. It had been almost a month since my box felt anything but solo action. Between finals and our work schedules, we never had time for a good fuck fest.

This was a first for me. Being held against a wall was a position I'd been wanting to try. I grinded my hips against his cock while he thrust into me. It was amazing. The thrill of the uncertainty of the situation made the sex that much better.

He banged into my pussy hard. It was obvious he'd been needing this as much as I had. In minutes, I was cumming. I could feel my juices drip out of me and knew he was getting soaked. The tight walls of my pussy convulsed and tightened around his cock repeatedly.

Chad's grunts were getting deeper, and I knew he was close to release. I braced myself for the quick pull out. He backed up, forcing his way through my locked ankles and lowered me to the floor. Grabbing my head, he thrust his cock into my mouth. With both hands on the back of my head, he fucked my mouth hard until he came, spewing cum into the back of my throat.

When he was through, I sat there smiling, wiping my mouth. They say hindsight is twenty-twenty. Looking back, it's obvious. The production when I walked in the room and wanting me to strip. Taking me against the wall which when I suggested it, he had said he wasn't sure about it because what if he dropped me or we fell. The forceful way he fucked my mouth was also new. There were no complaints from me about any of it, but where did he pick it up?

We showered together and decided against going out. Ordering a pizza while we recovered enough to go for round two was the plan. We got dressed to head to the living room while waiting on the pizza, maybe watch a movie. Chad turned to me wearing a red shirt, holding out the bottom hem like he wanted my opinion.

I pulled the corner of my mouth back almost instinctively, but tried not to frown. Red was not Chad's color. Green brought out his eyes. Blue wasn't too bad either. But red? Just no.

"What do you mean with that face?" he asked surprised. "You're the one who bought it for me."

That's when everything finally clicked. I didn't buy that shirt. I would never have bought him that shirt. When you start confusing your women, it never ends well.

"Who?" I took a deep breath

trying not to lose it. "Who is she?" I asked.

He looked at me, and I swear, there was no surprise in face. No 'where did that come from' defense. Nothing. "I thought you were the one who..." he stopped himself.

"How many?" I asked, my voice cracking.

Chad got this weird look on his face. I don't know how to describe it. Seemed like relief. Like he was glad to be caught, so he didn't have to keep up the lie anymore.

I slipped my shoes on and ran from his room.

He yelled after me, "Mindy, wait! Can't we talk about this?"

There was no defensiveness. No denying. There was nothing to talk about. My gut feeling was confirmed. Chad had been cheating. Part of me wanted to know the details, but I couldn't let him see me cry.

I grabbed my purse from the kitchen table where I tossed it when I arrived, and I was gone. I ran the entire way to my car. It wasn't that I thought Chad would come after me, but I didn't want to risk anyone else in the building seeing me lose my shit like that. By the time I made it to my car, the tears were streaming down my face.

I started driving home only that's not where I went. Without even realizing it, I drove to the Jacob's household. It wasn't until I pulled in the drive that it hit me what I had done. I decided just to stay. I let myself in the side door with my key and went up to the room I had there.

My parents are wonderful, but they're a little out of touch when it comes to relationships in today's world. It'd be better to have myself under control before I let them know Chad and I broke up. Plus, if driving home led me here, I guess that answered the question of whether I should take the position permanently. This house is apparently home to me now.

Chapter Two

Dear Diary,

Michael is in first grade which means I have my days free during the school year. I can get him off to school and attend classes of my own before having to be back at the house when he gets off the bus. Three of my classes are in the morning this semester. My other class is online. I try to get as much of my school work done as I possibly can before the bus drops him off in the afternoon.

The rest of the weekday evenings I do keep Michael preoccupied while Mark prepares his cases. He's a leading defense attorney in our county and charges a ridiculous amount of money just to answer an email. I have Sundays and every other Saturday off. It's not a bad setup considering I have free room and board plus a nice paycheck.

My room is actually a small apartment over the garage. It's perfect because I don't have to worry about waking Michael if I go out, and I can have friends over if I want without disturbing anyone.

Tara has been begging to go out with her and her boyfriend on a double date for a couple weeks now. I hate blind dates. The only reason I agreed to give up my free Saturday night for it is because I ran out of excuses not to go, and I know she won't shut up about it until I do.

Tara and Rob were picking me up, and Bryan is meeting us at the restaurant. Four more months till I can drink legally. Sucks!

I started getting ready for the date, but I misjudged my time. I was all dolled up with close to twenty minutes before they were supposed to be here. Somehow I got the time wrong. Seriously wrong. Now what?

Flipping on the TV, I started streaming the same show I'd been watching for weeks. That guy is damn hot, and I haven't had a fantasy that didn't include him since the night I first saw it. This episode was one of my favorites. Mmmmm... Makes my clit start to pulse just thinking about what's going to happen.

Oh, no. Dumb move. Why would I make myself this horny right before my date? Luckily, there was plenty of time to take care of matters.

I stood in front of the full length mirror and ran my hand across my chest and abdomen imagining the man from the show was standing close behind me. Slowly, I slid my panties off under short skirt and kicked them aside. I licked my first two fingers and started to rub them gently over my clit. The TV boomed in the background, and the sound of his voice helped me imagine it was his hand expertly guiding me to fits of pleasure.

Taking a step back, I reached into the nightstand drawer and took out my small stim. I pushed the button hopeful, and it still had a good charge to it. I put one knee on the bed, and started rubbing the stim across my clit. God, it felt amazing.

I leaned in and put my free hand on my bed giving the TV a quick glance. There he was. All six foot plus of pure handsome staring through the screen at me. A shiver went down my spine, and I closed my eyes. I rocked into the stim imagining him behind me taking me and filling me expertly. The tight walls of my pussy started to clench, and I moaned knowing release would soon be coming. I could feel my juice start to flow out and run down my inner thighs. One long guttural moan escaped my lips when my orgasm reached its peak, and I collapsed on the bed.

A noise startled me. I couldn't be sure what it was. Maybe I didn't actually hear anything at all. Maybe it was just a feeling that I wasn't alone. My eyes flew open, and there was Mark standing in the open doorway of my apartment.

I sprang off the bed and almost fell when my heel didn't quite land on the floor. Grabbing my bed to steady myself, I glanced down, and prayed my skirt was in place. Thankfully it was.

"I'm sorry," he said. "I was in the garage, and I thought I heard you yell."

I just stared at him, not knowing what to say. How much had he seen? How long had he been there?

"I'm sorry," he said again. "I'm going to go." With that, he disappeared.

Note to self. Make sure the door is locked before engaging in any fantasies.

After the interruption, I cleaned up and left with Tara and Rob. I must say the date went well. Tara had messaged me on the drive to the restaurant to say that she didn't think Bryan was my Mr. Right, but he could be right for one night.

She completely nailed it. He was handsome as hell. He had the body of an athlete, and I wanted to explore it. But when he opened his mouth, stupid fell out of it. There was nothing in his head at all.

It'd been a couple months since I had any dick, so I made a quick bathroom trip with Tara. The whole setup wasn't for romance at all. Tara knew I needed to get laid, and Rob had a friend who was a man whore. It was a win-win.

I let Bryan take me home after dinner and invited him up. My apartment wasn't much. It was basically one large room with a half wall that separated the small kitchen from the living area which was my bedroom. There was a private bathroom off the kitchen. When you open the door, the first thing you really see is my bed.

As I opened the door for Bryan, I looked at the exact spot where I had been earlier when I caught Mark spying on me, and my breath caught in my throat. It turned me on to know he may have been there when I came. That was enough. That one little thought, and I was ready. There was no sense in making small talk or dodging around the subject of sex with pleasantries for a while when Bryan and I both knew why he was in my apartment.

I shut, and locked, the door behind me then kicked off my

heels. Bryan was still eyeballing the place, slowly turning around full circle. By the time his gaze fell on me again, I was right beside him. I placed my hand on his chest and walked him back to my bed.

"Just like that?" he asked.

I smiled, "I know what I want."

He laughed. "I like that."

I didn't give him a chance to say anything more. I put my hand behind his head and pulled his mouth down to mine. He pulled his shirt up, and I broke the kiss long enough for him to rip it off over his head. Once again, I shimmied my panties down then pushed him back onto my bed.

Bryan undid his jeans and slid them down just far enough to

reveal his hard, thick member ready for action. I climbed onto my bed and straddled him. He reached under my skirt and carefully caressed the outer folds of my pussy.

"Damn, you're wet," he huffed.

"Moist like Duncan Hines," I smiled.

I moved his hand away. I needed his hard cock inside me. I started to guide it in then put both my hands on his chest while I sunk down allowing my pussy to swallow him. It wasn't until he was completely inside of me that I realized just how badly I needed this and how much thanks I owed Tara for helping me out.

Grinding into him hard, my

first orgasm came quickly. I knew it would. It had been too long.

Bryan cupped his large hands around my ass and forced me down on his hard cock over and over again. He was so thick, and I could feel his width stretch my walls apart every time his full length was inside of me.

He lifted his upper body off the bed, keeping hold of me on top of him until he was sitting up with me still riding him. Slowly, he managed to stand up and spun around as he did, throwing me on my back on the bed. He grabbed one of my ankles and lifted it over my shoulder with one hand while pulling me closer to him with the other. He started pounding into me hard, grunting with each thrust.

I knew he was getting close, so I worked my hand between us just enough to rub my clit trying to get one more in before he finished. I rubbed my clit just the way I like until I felt myself convulse, and my cum flowed down all around his shaft. Moments later, Bryan started to strain and let out one low groan before he pulled out and came on the bed.

It felt amazing having my pussy full of cock again. I vowed not to wait so long for the next time.

Bryan laid across my bed and started to get comfortable. I don't know what he thought was going to happen, but this wasn't it. I stood up and straightened my skirt and top. He reached for me, and I knew he probably wanted a kiss. Maybe he wanted to pull me down next to him. Fat chance.

"So, I have an early day tomorrow," I lied.

His eyes widened. "Oh...It's Sunday," he sounded surprised.

"Exactly. There's church in the morning." I figured it wasn't a terrible lie since there actually is church service on Sunday mornings, just none that I plan on attending.

Bryan relaxed a little and smiled at me. He patted the bed next to him, and said, "Well, we could always-"

I turned away from him and grabbed his pants and shoes. I

don't even remember him kicking them off. Handing them out to him, I said, "So, um, this was fun. Maybe we could go out again sometime."

That was a bold faced lie, but unfortunately, women learn early on that sometimes you have to side step the issue. It worked.

He started to dress and asked about how to contact me. I took his phone and sent a text to myself. With that, he leaned in and gave me a kiss before heading to the door.

I walked with him because I wanted to lock the door behind him. It was still up in the air if I would ever actually go out with him again, or if I'd have his number blocked before I went to bed. Either way, I didn't want him to conveniently forget something he left behind and let himself in to get it.

The stairs to my apartment went up the side of the garage off the walkway between the garage and the house. I stayed in the doorway longer than I had planned as he left. I'm sure Bryan probably thought I was watching him leave and probably took it to mean something that wasn't real.

It wasn't him I was looking at. For a moment, I thought I saw something on the darkened porch of Mark's house below. Straining in the darkness, I tried to see if I could tell what it was. It looked like something had moved, but now I figured it might just be my imagination.

Finally, I shut the door, still wondering about what I thought I saw. I frowned looking at my bed. I only had one set of bedding and now it was covered in Bryan's cum. I should be thankful he had the willpower and common sense to pull out since I was in such a hurry to get laid I forgot to grab a condom out.

I really wanted to take a shower, but I'd have to deal with making the bed first. I stripped everything off the bed, and bundled it up to take it to the house to wash. I could only hope Mark wasn't spending his Saturday night doing laundry. As I walked across to the porch, I scanned for what it was I might have seen, but there was nothing there except the two chairs and table on that side of the wrap around.

As quietly as possible, I entered the house through the kitchen. It wasn't that late, but Michael would already be in bed. The laundry room was empty, so I tossed everything into the washing machine and started it. I picked a shorter setting, but it would still be close to half an hour before it was done.

When I turned to leave, I almost screamed in fright. Mark was in the doorway leaning against the door jam. I hadn't heard him walk up, and seeing him there made me jump back into the washer. His eyes twinkled with delight at my reaction, and he took a couple steps closer to me.

He wore a pair of gray sweats and nothing else. Sweats that accented him a little too well in ways I had never paid attention to before now. It was all I could do to keep my eyes above his waist which wasn't much better given his muscled chest that was bared. I felt exposed, and I wasn't the one who was practically baring my all.

Once he was close enough that I was certain he could hear the rapid beating of my heart, he told me he didn't mean to scare me. He thought I'd heard him walk over. "Fun night?"

I stared at him, not sure what

he was asking.

"Well, this is from your bed?" he asked, pointing to the washer.

I nodded.

"And your friend just left?"

It hit me. It was Mark! That's what I'd seen on the porch. It had to have been him, but what was he doing out there? I nodded again.

"Well, it must have been fun if you can't wait until morning to get these cleaned."

I blushed, and I felt the heat in my cheeks just deepen and deepen.

Mark glanced me over from head to toe, and said, "It's alright. You're a big girl."

Something about the way he was looking at my chest when he said those last two words left me almost breathless.

"No need to wait," he added. "I'll throw them in the dryer for you, and text you when they're done."

I nodded and barely whispered, "Thanks," before edging my way past him and out of the house.

What was that? I asked myself as I left and have been asking myself ever since. Was he making some kind of move on me? That meant something, didn't it? It had to. Mark has never acted that way around me. Never.

I didn't see him again that night. He sent the text when the dryer was finished, but he wasn't around when I came to get my bedding. I found myself feeling... disappointed? I don't understand it. I've never seen Mark as a sexual object before, but there I was standing in his laundry room in a sexy nightie upset that he wasn't there to see it.

Chapter Three

Dear Diary,

I still can't quit thinking about Mark in those sexy ass gray sweatpants. Every time I see him now, I have to look away for fear he sees the flush in my cheeks. He haunts all my thoughts and is my only remaining source of fuel for my fantasies.

Now, I've had many nights where my mind started wandering, and I found myself wanting more in my bed to take care of me than any toy I owned. This is different. He is right there. Right next door. I find myself wanting to approach him, to proposition him, to just make myself available to proposition me if he desires.

This is not like me at all. I've never been one to chase after guys. Even when I've gone through dry spells in the past, I've let the guys come to me. Still, I find myself trying to make sense of what was going through his mind that night. Why would a man who's always in a suit, always pure business through and through, approach me in that way if he didn't want me? Was he feeling me out to see if I was interested in him? And why hasn't he made a move since?

Okay. It's only been two days. Maybe he will make a move again, but the wait is driving me crazy.

In fact, my thoughts and fantasies have been so filled with Mark that I need fulfilling. Bad. So much so that I made another date with Bryan. I had no intention of seeing him again after the night I met him. To me, it was a one night stand to take care of needs. I gave him my number to avoid a scene and get him out of my apartment. I had planned on blocking his number if he actually followed through and contacted me again.

As luck would have it, I was lying in my bed, getting off to thoughts of those gray sweatpants when Bryan called. It annoyed me at first: a most unwelcome interruption right when I was so close to climax. Almost immediately, I realized I might not be done with Bryan just yet. There may be cause for round two, and hopefully, I'll have Mark out of my system before there's a need for a third rendezvous.

I invited him over, and he was eager to accept. He had just left campus when he called, so it only took about ten minutes for him to knock on my door. He almost ruined the mood by talking before we finally got underway, and I started to regret answering his call.

It wasn't long before Bryan's hands were all over me. I closed my eyes and pictured Mark was the one exploring every inch. It wasn't easy with Bryan constantly carrying on about how much he wanted me and how he knew we were destined to be together. I came so close to telling him he was destined to go home with blue balls if he didn't shut his mouth.

After the last of my clothes were peeled off, I lay down on my back and pushed his head toward my mound. It was one way to shut him up. I placed my feet on his shoulders and grabbed the back of his head to pull his mouth even closer. I ground my pussy into his face and moaned while picturing those gray sweats and the bulge they showed off so easily in my mind. Damn, I wished it was Mark's face I was fucking.

A couple orgasms later, Bryan begged to come up for air. This time

I was thinking more clearly, and I grabbed a condom from the bedside table. The whole time I watched him while he put it on, I could only think I wanted this to be over. I wanted to go to the house to see if Mark was around. I knew I was going to have to do something about this absurd crush I suddenly had on him. Either offer my ass to him on a silver platter which could possibly get me fired, or I'd have to quit.

Bryan lowered himself on top of me, and I felt the sting of his thick cock enter me. My pussy remembered how much he had stretched me before, and it wasn't quite ready for another go with him. I bit my lip and rolled my eyes back and he filled me. He started off with long, slow strokes that gradually quickened until he was ramming me short and fast. Sweat beaded off his forehead and dripped onto my breasts. This is what I needed. I needed to be fucked hard.

"Damn, baby," he groaned. "You're pussy is fire."

I smiled mischievously at him. "She loves the feel of your cock." I told him and bucked up into him harder.

My moans grew louder and louder. There was no one around. No one to worry about hearing me. "Fuck me, Bryan!" I yelled out. "Harder! Make me cum!"

Bryan let out an animalistic

grunt then started to convulse as he came. The enlarging of his cock as he did pushed me over the edge, and I came with him. "Oh, God!" I screamed while the walls of my pussy hugged him tight and rained my cum down his shaft.

He rolled off of me and lay there for a moment before heading to my bathroom to dispose of the condom and clean up. By the time he came out, I was already dressed and ready for him to leave. The look on his face showed his disappointment.

"I'm not allowed overnight visitors," I lied. I realized it sounded stupid as soon as I said it. "In case the boy I babysit comes up here during the night. He sleepwalks."

I felt like a babbling idiot. I thought for sure anyone would see right through it, but I forgot how dense Bryan was. "Oh, okay. Yeah, I totally understand."

He grabbed his clothes and started pulling them on. He glanced at the television after he tied his shoes, but before he could make any suggestions, I had my hand on the door. "This was fun. Maybe we'll start earlier next time, so you can stay longer," I lied again. His number was being blocked tonight. There would be no next time.

Bryan smiled at me and sauntered over. "I'd like that," he said, leaning down to kiss me while I managed to wiggle the door open behind me.

As soon as the door shut behind him, I grabbed my phone and blocked him. While I was holding it in my hand, it dinged for a text notification, and I almost dropped it.

"Need to use the washing machine?" It was Mark.

Chapter Four

Dear Diary,

I can't quit thinking about the text Mark sent me a few nights ago. I never responded to it either. Part of me flew into immediate horror of how did he know what I had been up to, but I'm sure he saw Bryan's car parked outside. If Mark had been out on the porch, he may have seen Bryan leave. It made me feel like he was watching me.

It made me wonder if this would qualify as stalking. I always thought it would be terrifying to have a stalker, but it excited me to think that Mark was that interested in my sexual pursuits. It was equally surreal as this is not how Mark had ever acted before in all the years I'd known him.

Thinking back, I never paid Mark much attention. I suppose he's always been attractive, but he was also always a suit. He was strictly professional all the time. It was his wife, Jessica, who I'd talk to when arranging babysitting gigs and who would pay me. It was his wife who'd give me any necessary information run down before they left me with Michael, and she was the one who would ask how things went when they returned home. The truth is I hardly spoke to Mark or even much looked at him at all before she passed away.

That Mark is still very much present. I see him every morning when I come into the house before he leaves for work. He's the guy who walks through the door every evening, briefcase in hand.

It's just that occasionally now there's a different Mark who makes appearances. This Mark saunters around shirtless. Sometimes he wears gray sweats. He likes to sit on the porch on the side of the house facing my apartment after Michael goes to bed as if he's keeping an eye on me. He also spends a lot of time tinkering around in the garage when I'm home. I can hear him down there, and sometimes I wonder if his noise making is an attempt to lure me out to see what's going on.

That's absurd. I'm sure he's just finally starting to feel comfortable around me, so I'm finally seeing the relaxed side of him. Still, the relaxed side of Mark seems to be all I can think about now. Thoughts that make my cheeks blush whenever he looks at me as if I'm afraid he can read my mind.

Tonight I went to a campus party. I had to get away from the house for a bit. Parties on or near campus aren't my thing especially if any Frat jerks are going to be around. I'd much prefer a small get together, but I had to go.

My thoughts are so consumed by my boss. Every night I only sit around and try to think of reasons to head to the house in the hopes of bumping into him again. Without fail, the two nights I did muster the courage to go over, he was nowhere to be found. This wasn't healthy.

A couple friends picked me up and gave me a lift to the party. I'd could crash somewhere tonight, but I knew I'd probably take an Uber home. Tomorrow is my Saturday to work.

The party was typical. If you've seen one Midwest college party, you've seen them all. Barely dressed, barely legal college girls and loud music. Beer and shots everywhere, and the guys can do nothing but scream at each other as though it's socially acceptable male bonding.

I grabbed a drink and headed to the rear of the house, thinking I'd hang around by the pool. There was a small park that bordered the back yard, and it would be a quick escape if the police busted the party due to the volume.

It wasn't long before I was approached. Five minutes, maybe ten had passed before I heard a man's voice say, "You don't look like you're enjoying yourself."

I turned and the first thing I saw was gray sweatpants. My breath caught in my throat. Could it really be him? How did he find me? As I let my gaze travel upward, I realized it wasn't Mark.

"Oh, I am. Just lost in my

thoughts for a minute."

He smiled. He was handsome. I'll give him that. Tan with sandy blonde hair and blue eyes. He looked like he could've just walked off a movie set. "What were you thinking about?"

I started to answer then quickly realized I didn't want to play this cat and mouse game. I wasn't looking for a relationship. Finals were around the corner, and I needed to get my head straight about the man who was off limits for me. Nodding my head toward the back, I said, "The park."

His smile was dazzling, and he looked a little curious. "The park? Why?"

I shrugged. "It looks like a nice

little place. Not for kids. No playground equipment. But its well taken care of with walkways that crisscross a city block. Strange that it's here next to a Frat House."

Wow. Those words came out so easily, and even I was surprised. Every word was true, but not the normal conversation to have while trying to get buzzed at a party. I expected him to think I was some kind of nerd and take off.

"You're right," he said. "It is a little quaint which makes it seem out of place. Want to check it out?" he asked, extending his arm for me to take.

My lips turned up into a small smile. "My momma told me to never go anywhere with strangers," I teased.

"I'm Adam," he said and moved his arm to extend his hand.

I shook it, and said, "I'm Mindy. Pleasure to meet you."

"There. We're not strangers anymore, are we?"

"Guess not," I replied. I took a couple steps backward in the direction of the park. Adam was quick to follow.

We walked out of the backyard in silence then crossed through a side yard to get to the park across the street. It was empty, and with the help of a burned out street light on the south east corner, we would be hard to spot by any passerby once we were inside the gazebo. Curved benches lined both sides of the gazebo between the two entrances. It sat on one side of the park with a view of a statue that towered in the middle of the diagonal paths.

Adam and I walked straight to it. It's hard to say who led who there. Maybe we both desired the additional privacy knowing that even the dark of night wouldn't hide us completely. We sat on one of the benches close by each other, but not touching and leaned back against the rail of the partial wall behind us. Neither of us said much. We both wanted one thing, and we were equally uncertain how to instigate it.

It was a cool spring night, and it wasn't long before I shivered involuntarily. Adam slid over and put his arm around me. As soon as I turned my head toward him, he crushed my mouth with his. The taste of cheap beer was still on his tongue. His hands skillfully moved to my breasts, and I tried to let go and enjoy how he was making me feel.

Mark's face passed before my closed eyes, and I tried quickly to brush it out of my mind. I opened my eyes and broke free from the kiss. I reached down underneath his hoodie and grabbed the waist of his sweats, then felt for his bulge. I fumbled with his pants just enough that he helped by pulling them down for me.

He pulled his pants down just

enough to expose his rock hard cock then leaned back again. I knew he was wanting me to take control, so I climbed on the bench to kneel with my mouth over him. I let my tongue travel along the rim before taking the head in my mouth. I sucked on the head while teasing it with my tongue before slowly taking his length in my mouth. Not all at once. I bobbed my head up and down on his shaft taking in a little more each time until I had almost his full length in my throat.

A car could be heard coming down the road. When it turned, its lights shone in the gazebo and illuminated the opposite side. Adam and I dropped to the floor of the gazebo out of fear of being seen. Once the car had safely passed, he grabbed at my crotch through my skirt and began to kiss along the top of my breasts that squeezed out the top of my shirt. I unbuttoned the top few buttons until my entire bra was in view. He pulled down the material letting my tits bounce free and tugged on a nipple with his teeth.

I lifted my skirt and shimmied my panties down and off one foot, but they were still caught on my other ankle. I tried to reach for them, but Adam's large hand forcefully grabbed my bare pussy and began to push into it hard. He stuck two fingers into my pussy and rubbed my clit with his thumb.

I grabbed his wrist and pulled his hand closer almost wishing he'd drive more digits inside me.

He moved to the side and flipped me over, lifting my hips into the air to meet his groin. Adam continued to rub my clit while running his cock up and down inside the crack of my ass. For a moment, I thought he was going to try to fuck my ass dry. As he ran it down my crack one last time, he went even lower until the head of his dick caught the entry of my tunnel.

His hips circled as he teased my pussy before slowly leaning in and penetrating me. I gasped as he slowly spread me open. He wasn't as thick as Bryan had been, but what he lacked in girth, he made up for in length. He was at least seven inches fully erect, and he allowed me to feel every inch as it slowly made its way deep inside me. Once he was balls deep, he backed out just as slowly. Several times over, he took his time entering me then pulling back until he was out completely.

I felt him lean down over my back until he whispered, "Ready?"

"Mmm-hmm," I groaned, growing tired of being teased.

"Good." He placed one of his hands on my back just below my neck and violently forced me down until I was smashed to the floor of the gazebo. His cock entered me in one quick thrust, and he began fucking me hard and deep. I could tell he was close to hitting bottom, and it almost hurt each time he bucked against my ass.

His other hand trailed the length of my back until his fingers found their way to the rim of my ass. He teased my hole by tracing it lightly with his fingertips. Then he placed one finger directly on my hole and pushed it inside all the while not letting up on the damage he was doing to my pussy.

God, it felt amazing! I reached down and started rubbing my clit. I could feel my orgasm rising, and it was only a matter of moments. Adam could sense it too and wiggled a second finger into my ass. That was enough. I moaned loudly and felt my pussy convulse around his cock while my ass tightened repeatedly around his fingers.

I wanted him in my ass. His fingers was arousing the desire, and I wanted to tell him to take it. I didn't get the chance.

Adam began to grunt and buck wildly. I knew in a matter of moments he would be cumming. His grip on my back loosened just enough for me to pull away from him. I turned around quickly and took his cock in my mouth again. Less than a minute later, he was spewing his hot, sticky load down my throat.

I dressed rather quickly when we were down, not so much because of the chill in the air, but rather fear over getting a splinter in my ass. Adam laughed at me and told me the chances of splinters were slim. He somehow read my mind.

Turns out he really is a pretty cool guy. I gave him my number and actually hope he calls. Getting involved again so soon isn't what I had planned, but maybe he could get my mind off of Mark.

He was waiting for me when I got home on the porch again. I saw the faintest bit of movement in the darkness when I approached the bottom of the stairs. I took a deep breath, feeling the weight of his eyes wash fully over me. My every step was more deliberate and careful knowing I was being watched. When I reached the top of the stairs, I heard the screen door shut as he went inside.

Once in my apartment, I leaned against my door wondering how long he'd been waiting for me to get home and why. Was it just to make sure I was home okay? Or maybe to see if I was alone? Worst of all was it might not have anything to do with me. It might be a pure coincidence that he was even out there at all. I couldn't bear to think that for long. I wanted Mark Jacobs, and I needed him to want me too.

Chapter Five

Dear Diary,

Mark has me going crazy. It's been days without so much as a word from him, not a glance, nothing. Ever since the night of the party, he's been all business. I've tried to convince myself that he's busy with work, and he might have a big case he's working on right now. More importantly, I try to convince myself that it's for the best, and I should get on with my life.

That's exactly what I set out to do. Adam had been texting ever since the party, but he hadn't said anything to suggest he wanted to do more than send a few messages from time to time. Finally, I asked him over to watch a movie. This is what I was supposed to be doing. Going out with guys my age and having fun instead of spending all of my time obsessing over a guy fifteen years my senior.

The evening was going very well. He brought a bag of snacks over when he came, and laid across my bed to watch the movie. No other furniture to use, so we made do. I was surprised that he waited until after the movie to make a move. We started out as, and could just have easily ended as, a one night stand at a party. Yet, here he was with at least the illusion that this was more than just sex.

When it ended, we exchanged a few thoughts about how we liked the film before he leaned in for a kiss. He pushed me over on my back and kissed down my body until his head was between my legs, and he was kissing me over my leggings. He grabbed for the waistband, and I lifted my ass off the bed to allow him to pull them down. He pulled them completely down my legs then tossed them on the floor.

Adam lowered his head to my mound and lapped his tongue between my lips for a few moments before finding my clit. He teased it with his tongue and lips.

I started to moan and move my

hips beneath his mouth. With only the light from the television illuminating his face, the way his dark brown hair fell over his forehead, he looked like Mark.

'I've got to stop this,' I thought, closing my eyes. I rolled my head to the side. *'I can't keep thinking about him.'*

When I opened my eyes, I thought I saw Mark standing there, but it wasn't just fantasy; it was real. "What are you doing?" Mark bellowed, storming towards the bed.

I sat up and whimpered. I thought I was in trouble. Surely, I would be fired and would be evicted on the spot.

Instead, he marched straight to

Adam and tore the phone from his hand. Mark looked at it for a minute before showing it to me. Adam had been recording everything.

Adam scrambled off the bed to his feet. "It's n-n-not what you th-think," he stuttered nervously.

"I believe it's exactly what I think," Mark shot back as his fingers flew across the phone screen in an effort to delete the video. "Mindy is like family to me, and I won't have you coming in here disgracing her like this. Now, get out!"

"Y-yes, sir," Adam told him, reaching for his phone.

Mark went out the apartment door and stood on the landing at the top of the steps. He threw Adam's phone down to the driveway below. I could hear Adam's phone shatter as it hit and bounced across the pavement.

Adam didn't say another word. Mark came back inside. As soon as the doorway was empty, Adam made a run for it.

I knelt on my bed oblivious to how much of my body was exposed. Mark glanced at me then back at the floor. He grabbed the edge of the blanket and lifted it up, extending it to me to cover up.

"I apologize, Mindy," he said. "I wanted to see if you could come down earlier in the morning. The door must not have been shut all the way because when I knocked, it started to swing open."

I didn't say anything. I didn't know what to say. I couldn't even look at him.

Mark started toward the door then stopped. Without looking back, he said, "They're just boys, Mindy. Don't let them upset you. Someday, you'll know the difference between a boy and a man."

He continued toward the door. Just before he left, he added, "Forget what I said about the morning. You need your rest after this. Come down at the usual time." With that, he walked out of my apartment, leaving me horrified and alone trying to process everything that just happened.

Chapter Six

Dear Diary,

Days had passed since the night Adam was over. I had only left my apartment to go to work and school. There were so many unanswered questions.

What was Adam planning on doing with the video? Was it for personal use? Would it have wound up on social media? Was there some form of fraternity contest? Had my face ever been on the video? And most importantly, how had I not noticed it? How is it possible that he had a camera between my legs, and I didn't see it?

Did he record us at the gazebo as well? I tried not to think about that knowing how much easier it would have been to record us when he was taking me from behind. It probably would've been too dark to see anything which is the only comforting thought I had.

Mark and I had barely spoken since that night. When I finally collected my wits after he kicked Adam out of my apartment, I sent him a text simply saying thank you, but he never responded. There had been a few forced greetings in the morning and again in the evening when he came home.

This was the side of Mark I knew well. It was how all our interactions had been for the first several years I knew him. He had never been particularly friendly toward me. That's not to say he was ever rude, mean or treated me in any other negative way. Even with the occasional worry I entertained that I might lose my job, I felt like the worst case scenario from the aftermath of what happened with Adam was I missed my chance with Mark what with this strictly business side of him that seemed as though it was back for good. That's if I ever actually had a chance with him.

Partly, it made me feel like I was still in trouble. Or like he was disappointed in me. I worried that he might be considering replacing me because of it even though I knew I had done nothing wrong. It was my apartment. I was allowed to have friends and even boyfriends over. That had been discussed with Mark before I agreed to take the job full time.

I am an adult. It happened during my off hours. The only one who had done anything wrong was Adam. I suppose the argument could be made that Mark had also done something wrong by coming into my apartment unannounced, but if he hadn't? I don't like to think about if he hadn't.

It was my Saturday to work. Michael had a birthday party to attend this afternoon. I dropped him then came back to the house thinking I would get a load of laundry started before going back to pick him up. I went up to my apartment and collected my basket. In that short time before I came back out, Mark was once again sitting on the porch on the side of the house.

I walked down the stairs wondering why he so often sat on the side of the house. There was no view except for the garage and the steps leading up to my apartment door. That has to be the answer. He's watching my apartment. But why? And more importantly, should this be something that concerns me? Because it doesn't.

Without stopping, I said, "Hello," as I walked past him.

From the corner of my eye, I

could see him nod a greeting in response.

I pushed open the door to the house and went through the kitchen into the laundry room. There was a load sitting in the washer, so I transferred it to the dryer and started it before turning my attention back to my clothes. I filled the washing machine bin, added detergent and started it. When I turned to leave, I jumped. Mark was standing in the doorway. I hadn't heard him walk up.

He wasn't in the casual gray sweatpants, but he also wasn't in his professional work attire. He was dressed in a pair of khakis and a short sleeved button up shirt. I struggled in that moment, trying to remember a time when I had ever seen him in jeans, but I couldn't.

"When do you pick up Michael?"

I glanced at my phone to check the time. "I have about an hour before I go," I told him.

Mark looked off to the side and nodded, not so much as a reply to me. It was more as if he was nodding to himself over whatever thought was playing in his mind. He took a couple steps into the laundry room until he stood across from where I was with my back against the washing machine. "How have you been?" he asked, looking hard at my face.

"Good. Things are good," I lied, trying to sound as cheery as possible.

His eyes narrowed. "I mean it, Mindy. How are you?"

I shrugged and nervously looked away. "Okay, I guess."

He took a step closer to me. "I keep thinking about that night and what would have happened if I hadn't come in when I did," he said gently.

I could hear such a deep concern in his voice; I had to bite back tears. "Me too," I whispered.

Mark took another step closer. "The thing is, Mindy, I didn't come up to your apartment that night because I needed you to work early the next morning."

"You didn't?" I asked with a shaky, raspy voice. He was close enough now that I could feel the heat emanating off his body, and the physical effect his nearness was having on me was getting hard to hide.

"No," he shook his head. "I saw you go up with him, and I was jealous. I wanted to interrupt, to stop whatever evening plans you had. That's why I used my key to let myself in that night."

I gasped loudly. He had walked in on us! It turned out for the best, but what if Adam hadn't been such a creep? There'd be no excusing that kind of behavior then, and I'm sure my friends would argue it's still no reason to forgive him for what he did. No matter how much he does that borderlines or even crosses what is acceptable, I can't get angry with him.

"I hate to say it, but in that moment, I had the mindset that if I couldn't have you, I didn't want him to either. It worked out that I did go up there that night. It can't all be bad, can it?"

He spoke slowly, choosing his words carefully. As he explained himself, he continued to inch closer while examining my body from head to toe. My breathing became louder and faster. I wanted him closer, but I was too afraid to move. Afraid I'd break the spell, and he'd change his mind.

"No," I said, my voice barely above a whisper as I stared into his deep blue-gray eyes.

Mark leaned in to me, and his lips overtook mine. For the next several minutes, I was blissfully happy. Later, the fear and doubt set in as I thought about what had just happened more logically. For weeks, I have been wondering only about IF he was interested in me, IF he saw me as more than just a nanny, IF there might actually be something between us.

I never stopped to think about what if something DID happen between us. When it ends, and it most certainly will end, then what? He's fifteen years older than me. Even if that isn't an obstacle for him, do I really want a relationship with someone so much older, someone with a built in family? And the question causing the most anxiety is will I still have a job when it ends.

None of that mattered this afternoon in the laundry room. His tongue invaded every corner of my mouth while his hands roamed freely over my body, massaging my breasts over the light sundress I was wearing. I kissed him back as passionately as I could, grabbing his shoulders to pull him closer. My anticipation of this moment had been building for so long, and I felt like there was no time to waste. I needed him to fill me right then and there.

With one hand, I reached down behind him and cupped his firm ass both trying to pull him as well as will him inside of me. No matter how much I tried to shorten the small amount of distance between our bodies, he stood firm without moving an inch.

Mark broke free from my mouth and ran a trail of kisses down my neck, across my bosom, and over the front of my dress until he reached between my legs. Gripping my hips with both hands, he hoisted me atop the washing machine. He grabbed my panties and yanked them down my legs, tearing them off my ankles. He gently kissed my legs from knees to my inner thigh on both sides. Thinking about it now, I can still feel the heat from his breath on my skin.

Just before placing his mouth on my sweet spot that was screaming for him to taste me with every heartbeat that thudded in my clit, he looked up at me gingerly almost as if giving me one last chance to back out. I clasped my hands behind his head and pulled him to me. He circled my clit with his tongue then lowered his chin, driving his tongue straight into my wet pussy.

I lifted my legs and placed my sandaled feet onto his broad shoulders. Keeping my hands tight on the back of his head, I bucked into his face, grinding the heart of my passion into his mouth.

His tongue expertly darted between the folds of my pussy and my clit. Licking it furiously and grabbing it between his lips.

The washer began to spin out the water. I had to release one hand from his head to brace myself against the machine for fear of being bounced off. I continued to plow my hips straight into his face. My moans which had been soft at first began to escape me more freely when the realization that I didn't have to be quiet because no one else was home settled over me.

I was getting close to release, and expertly, he knew. He concentrated fully on my clit, devouring it until my bucking became more violent and uncontrolled as I came into his face. When my climax was over, he lowered his head again and sucked at the entrance of my labyrinth, savoring every drop that flowed out of me into his eager mouth.

He stood up, and I tried to pull him closer by his arms. He leaned back just out of arm's length. I straightened up on the washer and reached for his belt buckle. He grabbed my hands to step me and took a stop back away from me.

"No, Mindy, not here," he said, turning toward the door. "It matters that your needs are met; mine can wait."

He bent over and picked up my panties off the floor. I reached for them still unsure about what had just happened and what he meant by what he said.

Mark looked at my outstretched hand and smiled. "I think I'll hang on to these for a while," he said with a wry grin. He walked out of the laundry room, tucking my panties into his pants pocket.

I continued to sit there, dazed and uncertain, until I heard the door off the kitchen open and close. Hopping off the washer, I quickly ran to the window in the kitchen. I watched him get into his car and back out of the driveway. For several minutes, I stood in the kitchen with my mouth hanging open.

Never had someone so completely satisfied me without allowing me to touch them in return. Never had any of my partners not wanted some form of reciprocation. I know I'm in unchartered territory with Mark, and I can't wait to see what else he has in store.

Chapter Seven

Dear Diary,

It has been a week. It has been one entire week since the rendezvous with Mark in the laundry room. There has been almost nothing since then. I can count on one hand with room to spare the number of times that there has been any indication at all that he may have any interest in me.

The first time was one evening when I came around the corner in the hallway and accidentally bumped right into him. He leaned forward with his nose under my ear and inhaled deeply before side stepping me and moving on. Two days later after I tied Michael's shoes one morning, I stood up to see Mark standing behind his son. He gave me a wink. Then just yesterday, I was reaching for a glass in the kitchen when Mark walked passed me, caressing my ass as he went. Then he left the room as though nothing had happened.

That's been it. No texting. No emails. No calls. No late night visits to my apartment. No inviting me to his bedroom. No asking me to come over early in the morning or to stay late. Nothing.

I've been a mess trying to figure out what it means. Is it some kind of game he's playing? I mean who does that? Who eats a woman out like that then just walks away without any desire, much less demand, for reciprocation? I've spent all my free time this last week waiting and hoping there would be "something" from him. Waiting and hoping for round two if there ever will be a second round. Wanting to make sure I was available in case he finally showed interest.

Last night, I went to bed knowing that I was not going to waste my Saturday off doing more of the same. I woke up this morning and tidied up my apartment a bit. I finished my laundry yesterday to make certain I had no reason to go to the house today. I didn't want to invite the opportunity for him once again, only to have him ignore it.

I took a shower. Got dressed. I fixed my hair and did my makeup. I was set to spend the day out. I was going to do a little shopping. Maybe see if a friend was available for lunch. Anything. I didn't care what I did so long as I didn't spend the day in my apartment waiting on Mark.

It was as if he knew my limit had been reached.

My phone chimed as I was putting my shoes on to leave. I glanced at the screen. It was an image text from Mark. I opened my messages to find a picture of the panties he took last weekend laying on his bed.

Not sure how to respond, I sent, "Those look familiar."

Quickly he replied, "Would you like them back?"

My heart sunk. Does this mean it's over? Whatever "it" was. There wasn't really an "it" to begin with. And did I even want them back after he did god only knows what with them?

I was tired of it. Tired of the uncertainty. Tired of the games. Finally, I started typing a message in return. "There is a really cute bra that matches them, so yes."

I watched the three little dots dance at the bottom of the screen waiting to see what he said next. "Okay. But first, I have three questions for you. I want you to answer them all honestly."

More games. "Deal," I sent back. Then I waited again for the message to come across my screen.

"How many times in the last week did you think about me while you touched yourself?"

I sucked my breath in unprepared for how much it affected me to read those words. I could feel my temperature rise and the pounding in my clit immediately. But it was easy enough to answer. "Every time."

"No. How many times?"

"Every night," I replied. "Seven."

"Good." The dots appeared at the bottom of the screen again, and I found my thoughts wandering to what kind of sexual question was next. "For the second question, I sent you something in your email. I need you to watch it."

Curious, I closed out of my messages and opened my email. I found the one sent by him just a couple minutes earlier. I clicked on it, and there was a video attachment. I held my breath without realizing it until it started to play.

It was his home office. I could see a woman, closer to Mark in age, with short blonde curly hair and too much makeup. She was kneeling on the far side of the desk, smiling and waving at the camera while the camera was being positioned. I could hear her ask, "Is it good? Can you see me?"

His reply was muffled, but I recognized Mark's voice saying, "Yes."

She gave the camera two thumbs up.

Then I saw Mark come around the desk and sit in his chair in front of the kneeling woman. She smiled up at him while undoing his buckle.

'Oh my god!' I thought. *'Who is this woman?'*

She unzipped his pants and pulled his briefs down to release the largest cock I had ever seen in my life. With both her hands wrapped around his shaft, she couldn't cover his cock up to the tip.

My face flashed hot with anger.

I started scanning the screen for clues. I could see by the weather outside the office windows this wasn't very recent, but that wasn't enough to know when it occurred. Then I noticed a drawing Michael had made on the wall behind Mark's desk. I recognized it. I remembered pulling it out of his school bag the day he brought it home. He couldn't wait to show his dad. This video had to have been made since the start of this school year. It was long before I had any idea Mark was interested in me and before I had any designs on him myself. It didn't change how upset I was to see another woman enjoying the cock he hadn't yet let me experience.

The woman's head was bobbing up and down on Mark's rigid member. It was hard to see everything because of the desk, but it was obvious what she was doing. Mark leaned forward and grabbed her hair and yanked her head back off his cock. "Do you like that taste of my dick?" he asked her.

"Mmm-hmm," she moaned.

He thrust her head down on his cock. I could see her head twist from side to side, and I could tell her hands were working the shaft as well. He grabbed her by the hair again and forced her head farther down his shaft until she choked for a few seconds before yanking her head off him again.

"Suck my balls," he ordered.

She dutifully did as he requested. Her head dipped below the desk, but Mark could be heard giving instructions.

"First one," he told her. "Mmm, yes. Then the other. Now take them both in your mouth."

I could hear him moan. As mad and hurt as I was watching another woman give him pleasure, his moan turned me on. I could feel the throbbing in my clit, wishing I could take this woman's place.

They continued for several more minutes with the woman going to work on his cock. From time to time, he'd direct her on what to do using a handful of her hair to guide her or using her hair to pull her mouth down and ram his cock into her throat, choking her every time. It looked like she was getting off on how forceful he was. I knew I would get off to the memory of it later.

Finally, he grabbed her head with both hands and fucked her mouth hard. I could hear the muffled gagging noises she was making, but after several seconds, he threw her off him.

Mark took his dick in his hand and started jacking himself off. The blonde quickly recovered, kneeling before him with her head back and mouth open. After half a minute, maybe less, he shot his spunk at her. Some of it may have made it into her mouth, but her face was painted with his cum when he finished.

After zipping his pants, Mark walked around the desk. The video shook for a moment before ending completely. I stared at the black square on my phone screen, debating about pressing the watch again button.

The light on the top of my phone was flashing. I had a new message. I closed out of my email to read it. As I suspected, it was from Mark.

"Did it make you jealous?" he asked.

I stared at the message not wanting to answer. I felt dumb. It was stupid to be jealous when it occurred before I thought about Mark in this way and with some woman I don't know.

Then a second message appeared. "Remember. Be honest."

"Yes," I told him truthfully.

It took long enough to get another message that I began to panic I had given the wrong answer. There was no way Mark wanted something serious or long term with me. He would be looking for someone older, more settled, and more experienced. I'm sure he doesn't tolerate jealousy from his women.

"The woman in the video is a prostitute I saw a few times before I realized I had feelings for you."

'Feelings for me...What? He can't be serious.'

"Question #3."

My phone lit up, and I waited as he typed.

"Do you still want to fuck me?"

"Yes," I answered. That was the easiest of all the questions to answer.

"Then, these are yours," he sent. Next, he sent a picture of my panties hanging on my apartment door knob.

I jumped up and went to my door. Sure enough, they were there, hanging on the outside door knob. I looked around, but he was nowhere to be seen. I pulled them free and shut my door. How long since he left them there? How could he have put them there without me hearing him walk up the stairs unless he did it while I was in the shower? But that was over an hour ago.

Sitting on the bed, I kicked off my shoes without thinking about it. Somehow I knew my plans for the day were off. I wasn't going to get anything done now.

Chapter Eight

Dear Diary,

Mark and Michael pretty much disappeared Saturday and well into today. I don't know if they went on an overnight trip somewhere, or if they were just always gone when I went to the main house.

I had to work up my nerve the first time I went yesterday which wasn't long after his questions, but no one was here. After that, it became easier because he would have no way of knowing all the other trips I had made hoping to see him. Not just see him, of course. There were so many things

I wanted to do to him, but nothing was going to happen if I stayed in my apartment wishing for it.

After hanging out for most of Sunday afternoon in his living room, Mark and Michael came home. Temporarily. I was caught up in a television show I was binging and didn't hear the car. Michael had run through the kitchen before I was aware they had come in the door.

I grabbed the remote and paused the show. When I looked up, Mark was leaning his shoulder against the wall with his arms crossed. "Hello, Mindy," he said, raising an eyebrow.

"Sorry, I didn't hear you," I said. Then just as truthfully, "I came over to do some laundry." I washed my sheets again for about the fourth time this week, but I had started that load before noon.

"I think it's done," he said, glancing toward the direction of the laundry room.

I stood up and pointed to the television where my show was still paused. "Yeah, I may have got a little bit caught up in it."

Mark didn't follow me into the laundry room. I was a little disappointed given that I had heard him send Michael upstairs to put his things away. Part of me hoped he had sent Michael out of the room to give us a few minutes alone. I switched my clothes into the dryer now regretting not having finished them earlier. I was going to be stuck here close to another hour waiting on my bedding to dry before I could go home and relax in my own tiny apartment where the only furniture was my bed, and the worst part was it didn't even need washing. It was just my excuse to bring me to the main house. I began to consider just going home and sleeping on my bare mattress tonight.

After starting the dryer, I walked into the kitchen, but I didn't see anybody. It was probably better that way anyway. I would hate for Mark and I to be in the middle of something only to have Michael come running into the room. That poor boy had already been through enough.

I grabbed a glass out of the cabinet and took it to the refrigerator to fill it with ice and water. It was a combination of being lost in my thoughts about not wanting to hurt Michael and the noise of the ice maker that caused me not to hear Mark sneak up on me.

He grabbed me from behind, wrapping his arms around me and pinning my arms to my sides in the process. I felt his mouth on my neck, and the heat in my body rose immediately. He whispered, "We don't have much time."

I leaned to the side to set my glass in the counter, hoping he'd free me from his embrace allowing me to turn and face him. Instead, he pushed me hard from behind, completely pinning one arm to the counter. My other hand was free, but pretty much useless with his arm still holding it tight to my side.

Mark continued to kiss and nibble on my ears and neck, going from one side to the other, and back again. I could feel his hot breath everywhere on my exposed skin. He leaned into me harder, forcing my upper body to bend further over the counter. He unwrapped his arms from around me, but I was still pinned on one side. The other arm, he continued to hold to my side with one hand. With his free hand, he pushed my upper back down until I was fully bent over with my head carefully tucked under the cabinets. Keeping me still in that position, he let my one arm free which I used to brace myself as I was standing on the very tips of my toes in a position I knew I wouldn't be able to hold much longer. My panties were already soaked from my pussy that was eager for attention.

I thought for sure any minute now Michael's little feet would be heard as he came running back this way. I would be left high and dry, headed home. In my apartment, I'd take matters in my own hands.

Mark's free hand slowly caressed my ass, cupping each cheek with a tight squeeze. I could hear him let out a moan of approval. Leaning into me, I could feel his hard cock through the khaki material of his pants press against my ass. I have never desired a man so much in my life.

He lifted the back of my skirt and toyed with the material of my thong, hooking his finger underneath and running it along the small piece of fabric. He expertly slid the thong down without unpinning me. Sliding his hand over my ass once again, he didn't stop until his fingers reached my wet pussy. He began rubbing me with his fingers before inserting one, then two inside me.

Leaning close to my head again, he whispered, "Are you mad at me?"

"No," I choked out.

"You're not mad about the video?" he asked.

I moaned out, "No." The walls of my pussy tightly squeezed around his experienced fingers.

"Do you know why I sent that video?"

"To make me jealous," I breathlessly answered. The pitch of my voice going up as I spoke while his fingers roamed their way through my love tunnel, bringing me closer and closer.

I could hear him chuckle behind me, "No, my sweet."

Behind me, I could feel Mark either kneel or squat, and his breath covered my ass. I was preparing for another one sided session of being ate out without giving him anything in return. We didn't have enough time.

It caught me off guard when I felt his tongue on the button hole of my ass. He ran his tongue in circles around my ass hole gently, stirring sensations I had never felt before now. His tongue pressed against my tight hole, trying to penetrate with little luck. With his other hand, he traced a finger around the track his tongue had just laid down. The tip of his finger touched the center of my hole. He pushed ever so softly until it penetrated my ass.

That was enough. Between the way he was owning my pussy and

now playing with my ass, I had reached mine. I started to moan, and I could feel my whole body convulse as the shockwaves of my orgasm traveled through me. He continued to fuck both my pussy and ass with his fingers as I came, allowing me to ride my orgasm higher and higher and higher.

It wasn't until after my orgasm had finished, and my body had stopped jerking and twitching that I could feel his mouth. He was between my legs sucking the entrance of my labyrinth, savoring all the juices that flowed out of me.

When he stood up, he spun me around to face him, crashing his mouth on mine for a kiss. He told me he had wanted to do that again all week. A noise could be heard upstairs, and we knew Michael was on his way.

Mark turned back to me and smiled, "Perfect timing," he said. "I guess I better go get ready for dinner myself. I'll see you soon," he said with a wink. Then he gave me one more quick kiss before leaving.

Later after getting my bedding from the dryer, I was back at my apartment in my freshly made bed, snuggled under the covers watching a movie. It was a stupid rom-com that I've seen over a hundred times already. My phone chimed, and it was Mark.

He sent several texts explaining he sent me the video because of what happened with Adam. I would probably find out about them eventually, so he wanted to tell me himself instead of me finding out about them accidentally. The same goes for his history with prostitutes. He wanted to be the one to tell me.

At the end, he added, "Don't worry. I would never record anyone without their permission, including and especially you."

I held the phone to my chest and stared at the ceiling for a long time. I thought about it wondering how long it would be before he asked me.

Chapter Nine

Dear Diary,

It's finally Friday. I've been looking forward to tonight all week. There hasn't been a single opportunity for Mark and I to be alone since that day in the kitchen. It's frustrating because by the time Michael falls asleep, Mark has to get to bed because his job is so demanding. There's been signs though. He's given clues that he's still into me.

The last several days have shown me that I can expect big things this weekend. Mark invited me over to dinner one night, and another night, the three of us watched a movie together. We couldn't do anything, not even snuggle on the couch. I get that he doesn't want to let his son know anything is going on yet. I do. But being a secret does nothing to increase my confidence about how serious Mark is about me. Does he really just want to wait to tell Michael? Or is it that I'm someone he's never going to tell his son about?

In addition to the extra time we spent together, he would sneak a touch or caress whenever he could. He might cop a feel when Michael was distracted or rub my ass when I passed. I received texts often telling me how beautiful I looked that day, or how he couldn't wait to ravage my body.

But today was the day. Michael had a four day weekend from school. His grandparents picked him up this morning and took him for a long visit. I had been looking forward to today ever since I found out Michael would be gone. It was no use to try not to get excited or wonder about what Mark might have in store. I knew I was setting myself up to be let down, but I couldn't help it. Turned out that I had nothing to worry about. Sort of.

Mark had made no definitive plans, but he did tell me he was looking forward to spending time with me tonight alone. He had sent texts all day from the office, making sure I didn't have plans. He also told me what time he should be home and that he hoped I would be there waiting for him.

When he walked in the front door of his house, I was sitting on his sofa, snuggled in a blanket and watching television. Mark looked at me and smiled, "Comfortable," he asked.

I looked at him and nodded.

"Have you ate? Are you hungry?"

I smiled mischievously, "Oh, I could eat."

Standing up, I let the blanket drop to my feet revealing to him that I was nude from head to toe.

Mark's suitcase dropped to the floor at his feet, and he began loosening his tie. "Suddenly, I feel famished," he grinned, moving toward me.

We met each other halfway. He wrapped his arms around me, picking me up off the floor as his lips found mine. His tongue explored my mouth passionately. He carried me down the hall to the stairs where he set me back on my feet.

I walked backward up the stairs while our hands were soon all over each other's bodies. Mark tore his suit jacket off not removing his mouth from mine. Then he was cupping my ass with one hand and one of my breasts with his other. I frantically worked on the buttons of his shirt while trying to pull it up and free it from the waist band of his pants blindly unable to see what I was doing.

Mark and I continued slowly up the stairs. HIs mouth ran a warm stream of kisses from my ears, over my neck, to my breasts. Both of us wanting. Both of us eager. I lost my footing and fell backward on the stairs, erupting in laughter at my clumsiness. Mark came down on top of me. His mouth encircled one breast, sucking my nipple and teasing it with his teeth. I finally managed to get the last button of his shirt undone when his hand found my sweet mound.

His fingers opened the folds of my pussy and teased the entrance of my tunnel. I gripped the back of his neck with one hand, keeping his mouth firm on my tit. My other hand I used to brace myself on the step for balance. I felt one of his fingers slip inside me, and my head fell back with an involuntary moan of approval. It was followed immediately by a second finger, delving the walls of my pussy. I grinded my hips into his hand while his fingers dug deep inside me.

Within minutes, I had reached my climax. My hand relaxed on the back of his neck, and he looked at me deeply, watching the pleasure that was written on my face. When my orgasm ceased, he kissed me again before suggesting we take it to the bedroom.

He helped me to my feet, took my hand, and led me the rest of the way up the stairs, down the hall to his room. Once inside, we walked to the bed where he gently pushed me back on it. I laid there and watched as he kicked off his shoes then undid his belt and pants. He let his pants slide off then he pulled down his boxer briefs, letting me see his massive cock in person for the first time.

I sucked in my breath, shocked. Even though I had seen it on video, it didn't compare to how massive it was in real life.

He placed one hand on the bed to support himself while he reached down with the other, removing the rest of his clothing. He came down over me and scooped me up with one large hand under my back, scooting me farther onto the bed until we were fully laid sideways across it.

Mark kissed every inch of my body, beginning with my ears to my neck, down to my breasts, across my mid-section until finally reaching my sweet spot. His tongue devoured the folds of my pussy and teased my clit briefly until he lifted back up, positioning his body over mine. He kissed my lips gently and whispered, "Are you ready?"

"Oh, yes," I said a little too eagerly.

He smiled, and I could almost hear a faint ghostly chuckle. He poised himself over top of me, pushing his tip into my pussy, and I moaned loudly. He paused and looked at me. "Okay?" he asked.

I grabbed his shoulders and tried to pull him inside my box. He leaned into me. His girth demanded the walls of my pussy give way to make room.

The cries that came forth from my throat were foreign even to me. Mark stopped again. "You alright?"

"D-don't ... stop," I uttered between raspy breaths.

With one more powerful thrust, he was balls deep. The cry emitting from me was almost a scream. "Damn! You feel wonderful." I moaned, wanting to beat him to the punch of asking me if I was okay for a third time.

He pulled back until he was almost all the way out then slowly leaned his full length back inside. His rhythm increased with each thrust until he was pounding into me hard.

My moans became a constant cry that rose louder and louder. The walls of my pussy convulsed constantly contracting all around his massive cock as my juices flowed. One orgasm after another. It was hard to tell when one ended and another began.

He propped himself on his elbow and reached down to play with my clit while thrusting into me. My cries reached a pitch so high I had never before heard it come from my mouth. The pleasure was so intense it was almost painful. When I had reached all I could take and wanted to beg him to stop, I felt his size swell inside of me and knew he was close.

Mark began to buck and twitch. I felt him cumming deep inside of me, and I could feel the warmth of his load coat my love tunnel.

He collapsed on his side next to me. Both of us tried to catch our breath for minutes afterwards unable to speak. We went several more rounds before the night was over. When I was so spent I could barely walk because my legs were shaking so bad, all I wanted to do was collapse in his arms and rest.

That's when he told me he had an early start in the morning. He had to meet clients out of town for an important breakfast meeting. He'd be leaving at an ungodly hour and would be up much earlier to get ready. He told me I could stay if I wanted, but it might be better if I went home where I could get more rest without being woke by him so early.

I didn't want to go home. I wanted to stay in his arms for the entire night even if I would be asleep and unaware of a minute of it. I just couldn't shake the anxious feeling that he was trying to get rid of me. I don't like being where I think I'm not wanted.

So I'm home where I will lay in bed tonight and cry myself to sleep. Whatever plans Mark has for me, they certainly aren't long term. He's not at fault. He never gave any indication that this would amount to more than an affair. Hell! He showed me a video of him with a prostitute. That should've been a big enough warning flag right there.

It bothered me that he wasn't seriously interested, and there could be only one reason why. I was falling for him. That was something I never expected to happen and didn't see it as it was developing until now. I was caught up in feelings for Mark – hook, line, and sinker. This wasn't going to end well. However long it lasted, whether it be weeks or months, I would walk away from this house for good with a broken heart, no job, and no place of my own to live.

Chapter Ten

Dear Diary,

I slept late today. When I woke up, my body screamed at me while I tried to get out of bed. Every muscle in my body ached, but especially all the muscles from the waist down. I managed to sit on the edge of the bed, but every time I tried to stand, my legs would shake and were too weak to support me.

It took what seemed like forever, but was probably only ten minutes. I used the wall for support and managed to make it to the bathroom. A shower was the top priority. I let the steaming hot water cascade all over my body in the hopes of soothing my muscles. It might have helped a bit. My legs stopped failing me so much. But as the water flowed across me, I felt Mark's mouth on my skin, exploring my body.

The sensations my fantasies stirred were exquisite, and I wondered if I would experience them in real life again. Surely, he wasn't done with me yet. The thought was bittersweet. I wanted Mark completely, but I knew he didn't feel the same in return. My only option was to enjoy his body as long as he would allow me.

I peeled myself away from the shower and dried off. Mama always said, "You never know what the day might bring." So I went ahead and took care of my hair and makeup. Nothing too fancy as I only planned on laying around watching movies all day.

Deciding what to wear took longer. I wanted to lounge in sweats, but if something came up, I didn't want to spend the time changing before leaving. Not because I might be in a hurry, but because I didn't want to move. I chose a cute dress instead. It had a built in bra support which meant I wouldn't have to wear anything at all underneath. Dressed for company and very comfortable.

I turned on the television and found something to occupy my time. It wasn't long before Mark sent a text.

"I've got a surprise for you."

"What is it?"

"You'll have to come over and see for yourself," he insisted.

Oh, man. The curiosity over what the surprise might be almost wasn't enough to get me to want to move my body down those stairs. But I went. Of course, I went.

I slipped on a pair of ballerina shoes and headed out the door. The stairs weren't as menacing as they looked. Soon I was on the path that connected the house to the garage. I opened the side door into the kitchen and softly called out, "Mark."

No answer.

I walked through the dining

room, across the front of the house into the living room, but I didn't see him. I left the living room and stood near the entrance of the house wondering where to look next. Maybe his office down the hall in the back of the house?

While I was thinking, Mark called out from upstairs, "Mindy?"

"Yes."

"Up here."

"Easier said than done," I mumbled. I walked up the stairs slowly, but I could feel myself growing stronger with each step I took. At the top of the stairs, I turned left and walked down the hall toward his bedroom, knowing that's where he had to be. The door was partially open, and the light poured out into the hall.

Standing at the doorway, I pushed gently until the door swung all the way open. I could see Mark wearing nothing but his boxer briefs setting up a camera on a tripod near the bed.

"Hello beautiful," he said when he saw me. He walked over to me, throwing his arm around my waist to pull me close for a soft, sweet kiss. "I've almost got it ready."

"A video camera?" I asked.

He stopped mid-step and turned back. "If it's alright?"

I shrugged, thinking I had never knowingly been videotaped. If any of the guys from my past had asked me, I probably would have freaked out over it. With Mark being a lawyer, I didn't feel like there was any reason to worry about him doing something devious with the tapes later.

"No," he said sternly. "You have to tell me. Is it okay? A shrug is not an answer."

"Yeah, I mean I've never done it before," I told him, shrugging again absent mindedly then laughed. "It's okay. Yes. It's fine that you record us."

"Okay then," he said, continuing back to the camera. He fidgeted with it for a little bit more then said, "There. I think it's perfectly in frame."

"Now what?"

He shimmied his boxer briefs down his legs and kicked them off revealing his semi erect cock. "Now? Whenever you're ready, I push record, and we begin."

I looked at the bed for a moment before grabbing the skirt of my dress, bunching it up with my fingers. Once I got hold of the hem, I lifted it all the way up and over the top of my head and tossed it to the floor, revealing my nude body underneath. "Ready," I smirked.

Mark looked over my body slowly, fucking me with his eyes. Then his gaze met mine, and he grinned, "Ready."

He pressed the button on the camera then came to me and grabbed me, pulling me toward the bed where I fell down on top of him.

Pushing down with one hand on the bed for support, he maneuvered us around until we were laying in the position he wanted, keeping me pressed to his chest the entire time.

Once he was satisfied we were angled correctly for the camera, he lifted his head toward me, and his mouth found mine. He locked our lips in a kiss and gently eased me off him to the side. Cupping one breast then the other, he rolled my nipples between his fingertips, making them taut. Then he slid his hand down between my legs where he began teasing me, roaming his fingers through my folds, slipping a finger inside then back out to explore my pussy lips again.

The way the camera was angled I knew my pussy was on full display. The thought crept into my mind of him watching the tape later while pleasuring himself. It turned me on, and I had to break from the kiss to allow my moan the freedom to be heard.

He pulled me back on top of him and pushed against my shoulders until I was sitting on his lap. I balanced my weight on one knee, and reached down, wrapping my hand around his now fully erect cock. I used my other hand to part the folds of my pussy and brought the tip of his dick up to meet my entrance. I slowly slid down his cock, not far. I lifted back up and did it again, allowing him to slide in a little deeper this time. I repeated this over and over until I had finally managed to take his length completely.

My pussy was sore and tired from last night, and it screamed its objections at me when his cock first began to enter me. By the time I took his full size, it had a change of heart and was eager for more. I rode him, grinding into him more gently than he had fucked me last night, not wanting to risk it becoming too painful to enjoy. I reached my first orgasm quickly, and then my second just as effortlessly. After the third or fourth time I came, Mark pulled me down to him until I lay flat on his chest, and kissed my neck, whispering into my ear, "My turn."

Carefully, he moved me off of him onto the bed, keeping me on my stomach. He straddled my legs and entered my pussy from behind. He continued my slow, gentle strokes until he easily manipulated another orgasm.

"Are you ready for more?" he asked.

I moaned, "Oh, yes."

Mark chuckled softly behind me. "I don't think you understand the question."

Before I could ask what he meant, I felt his finger trace the edge of my butt hole, and I sucked my breath in at the thought of taking him in my ass.

He leaned closer to me, and

said softly, "But I see you're a fast learner."

"Mark," I started to object. My body instinctively tensed up as my apprehension grew.

His hands caressed my full ass while he continued to thrust inside my pussy. "Do you trust me?"

I hesitated to answer. I did, but I was afraid.

"Mindy?"

"Yes."

"Do you?"

I still wasn't sure how I felt about it, but I answered, "Yes, I trust you."

Mark wiggled a finger inside of my ass with ease and fucked my tight hole with it. He pulled on the rim of my ass with his finger from all sides, trying to loosen me. "Relax, Mindy. You need to stop tightening these muscles."

I tried. I really did. As soon as I started to relax, I would think about his thick nine inch cock ripping my ass open, and I'd tense up again.

"Have you tried anal before?"

Once again, I hesitated. I didn't want him to think of me as inexperienced.

"Other than playing around like this? Mindy, have you ever taken a cock in your ass?"

I still couldn't form the words to answer him, but I did manage to shake my head, "No."

Mark pulled out and moved off me. Within seconds, he was

walking across the room.

I couldn't bring myself to watch him. I knew he was turning off the camera. This was done. We were done. He was disappointed that I didn't wind up being the wild ride he had hoped I would be. I let him down, and it was over. My eyes started to water, but I squeezed them shut tightly, refusing to allow a single tear to hit my cheek.

After a couple minutes passed, I felt him return. The mattress caved under his weight, and I knew he was near me again.

"Mindy," he said, shaking my shoulder gently. "Hey, everything alright?"

I lay frozen like a statue. I couldn't speak because I knew my voice would crack. If I faced him, I knew he'd be able to see how close I was to tears.

He sat near my head and tried to pull me into his lap. I resisted, but he managed to win out. With my head on his leg, he stroked my hair. "If you don't want to, we don't have to."

"I want to," I said, barely above a whisper.

"Then what's wrong?"

I rolled off his leg and sat up, facing away from him. "I'm afraid it's going to hurt."

Mark laughed. It started small, but built into a full gut busting laugh. "I'm sorry," he said repeatedly, between fits.

Finally, he tapped my arm with

something. When I ignored it, he tapped me harder. I looked down to see a large bottle of anal lube. He was holding it out to me, so I took it, looking the bottle over carefully.

"Let me explain something to you," he said, pulling himself over to my side. "I'm an ass man. Always have been. But I want you. If you don't want to do it, I won't pressure you. And, I'll still want you."

"Really?" I asked.

He took my hand and kissed it. "I swear. It probably will hurt especially if it's your first time. That's why I got the lube. You won't be ready for anal without it for a long time."

Mark sat up and put his hands on either side of my face, looking deep into my eyes. "Now, if you want to try it, we can. If it's too painful, I'll stop. If you're not ready, that's cool too."

I looked back down at the lube. I was scared to death. Friends of mine had tried it, and none of them had ever said anything good about it. As scared as I was, I wanted to please him more than I was afraid. "I want to try," I sighed, trying to force a smile.

He grinned at me and came in for a full, passionate kiss. When he broke it off, he reassured me, "At any time you want to stop, I'll stop. I promise."

I believed him.

Mark laid me back down on my stomach and came around behind

me again.

I felt the coolness of the lube run down over my ass into my already wet pussy. His fingers scooped it up, and gently pushed it into my tight ass. He guided his fingers in and out several times slowly.

"Mmmm," he moaned. "I can't wait to be your first, Mindy. Are you ready?"

"Yes," I answered, barely loud enough for him to hear.

He removed his fingers, and I heard the lid of the lube snap again. I couldn't see him. I couldn't try to look, but I could tell by what I heard that he was rubbing it over every inch of his cock.

I felt the tip of his massive shaft

press against the button of my ass. It turned me on significantly more than what I was already feeling. My breath caught, and I tensed up, waiting for him to enter me.

"Relax, Mindy," he told me gently.

I tried. I relaxed as much as I could.

Mark leaned forward, and his tip entered me. Then he pressed a little more, and a searing pain shot through my ass. I bucked forward away from him out of instinct.

"Trust me?" he asked.

"Completely," I said. I did trust him, but I was scared to death.

He grabbed my hips and positioned me again. This time he held onto them tightly as he slowly drove his cock into my tight ass. I couldn't move away.

The pain was intense, and tears formed in my eyes. He barely made any head way before he pulled out and entered me again. It took several attempts before he managed to fit his entire length inside of me.

"God!" I cried out. I felt like I was about to rip open. It was excruciating and exciting at the same time. Pleasure and pain in each slow thrust of his cock.

"That's my girl," he said breathily, sliding in and out. His movements were still slow, but he was starting to pick up his speed.

He leaned over my back and reached one hand around to my

clit. Using his thumb, he circled it tenderly. As he built up his deep thrusts into my ass, he picked up the tempo on my love button as well.

"Oh! Oh Mark!" I screamed as I came. The tight walls of my pussy convulsed, and the walls of my ass tightened around his cock.

"Yes, Mindy," he moaned. "Let your body show me how much you love my cock in your ass."

"I do, Mark," I said between gasps. I meant it. I had never felt so fulfilled.

His rhythm quickened until he was thrusting into my ass just as hard as he had previously rampaged my pussy. The lube was wearing off, and it was starting to hurt more and more with each thrust. I didn't care.

Even when his hand slipped away from my clit, I didn't care. I wiggled my arm underneath and took over for him. I wanted him in my ass. I didn't want it to stop. I knew he was about to cum, but I didn't want it to ever end.

Mark's body began to twitch, and I felt his cock grow inside my ass right before he came. I felt each drop of his hot cum shoot inside me.

He collapsed on top of me and asked if I was okay.

"Only if you promise me one thing," I told him.

"What's that?"

"Promise you'll do that again...

And often."

Coming Soon

Stay tuned for more installments of the Nanny Diaries and Family Secrets series by Darling Coxx! Family Secrets #1 expected October 1, 2021!

More by Darling Coxx
Nanny Diaries #1

Lacey Moore bit off more than she could swallow when she took the position at the Wyndham estate. What was supposed to be the perfect job accompanied by great hours, pay and perks like living rent free in the guest house soon turned out to be more than she had could have ever imagined. The main duties of her job included making sure the entire staff stayed satisfied, and it was a job she intended on doing well.

Nanny Diaries #2

Vicki Sweet didn't know what she was walking into when she took the job as nanny for the Rayburn's. Soon she found herself loaded with maid duties as well as chasing after the children while Lance worked and ignored all of his wife's illicit activities. Tori Rayburn needed to be put in her place, and Vicki was just the woman for the job. Chasing after Tori's affairs, Vicki began stealing them away one by one, but her eye remained on the ultimate prize. Vicki would have her saucy way with Lance before her job ended, and once she set her mind on something, she always got what she wanted.

About the Author

Darling Coxx is a seasoned writer who has been featured in many major publications under her given name. Taking a break from interviews and personal experience pieces, she is trying her hand at short novellas in the same genre she's been working in for most of her life.

Her adult entertainment career began while working as the manager of an adult store. It is her favorite position of any she's held, before or since. It was there where she made the contacts that allowed her to venture into the world of adult entertainment both in her own writing as well as producing a few pieces of her own.

Please feel free to reach out to her at DarlingCoxx@gmail.com. Follow her on Instagram @DarlingCoxx to stay updated on future publications. And don't forget to subscribe to her OnlyFans account @DarlingCoxx.

www.ingramcontent.com/pod-product-compliance
Lightning Source LLC
LaVergne TN
LVHW032010070526
838202LV00059B/6383